Winter Wonderland

Written by Judy Katschke
Illustrated by Prescott Hill

Scholastic Inc.

ISBN 978-0-545-60779-7

Published by Scholastic Inc. SCHOLASTIC and associated logos are trademarks and/or registered trademarks of Scholastic Inc.

10 9 8 7 6 5 4 3 2 1 14 15 16 17 18 19/0

Printed in the U.S.A. 40
First printing, December 2014

Contents

Chapter 1
Snow Problem

"Thanks, Blythe!" Penny Ling the panda said, scooping pawfuls of snow. "This field trip to the park is the bestest ever!"

"And the coldest." Sunil Nevla the mongoose shivered.

Blythe Baxter smiled at the day campers, bundled up from head to tail.

"It is cold," Blythe agreed. "But you guys look totally cool in my Blythe Style winter fashions!"

The pets smiled, too. Blythe was the

best thing to happen to Downtown City's Littlest Pet Shop since gourmet pup-cakes. Blythe understood the pets when they spoke, she designed awesome clothes for them, and she and her dad lived in the apartment upstairs, just a quick ride up the dumbwaiter.

"Who's up for building a snow-pet?" Blythe asked.

"How about a glam snow-pet with cutting-edge style?" Zoe Trent the Spaniel said, striking a pose.

"And we can call her . . . Zoe?" Pepper Clark the skunk teased.

"Let's build a snowy hot fudge sundae!" Penny said.

"Not too hot," Vinnie Terrio the gecko said, "or it'll be a hot fudge slushie."

But Minka Mark the monkey was impatient.

"Chaaaaarge!" she shouted, racing up a hill. Once on top, she began to sculpt, snow flying everywhere!

When Minka was done, the pets *ooh*ed and *ahh*ed. She had turned a lump of snow into a statue of Blythe!

"Thanks, Minka." Blythe smiled. "I promise not to let the fame go to my head." Then—

WHACK, WHACK!! Two snowballs knocked the head off of Blythe's statue.

"What the—?" Blythe gasped.

Chapter 2
Cold Shoulder

Blythe and the pets whirled around. There, dusting snow off their fashion-forward gloves were Whittany and Brittany Biskit!

"Hello, Blythe." Brittany sniffed.

"Having fun with the . . . creatures?" Whittany said.

"We were," Blythe said. "Until things got . . . icy."

"Like, here!" Whittany said, shoving a flier in Blythe's face. It showed a man with styled hair, holding clippers.

"Mr. Kenny?" Blythe read out loud.

"Known as the dog groomer to the stars!" Whittany bragged. "And as of today, he's the official groomer at our father's store."

"Largest Ever Pet Shop!" Brittany bragged.

As if Blythe didn't know the name of Fisher Biskit's oversized pet store. It was big on stock but small on heart.

"Mr. Kenny came just in time to celebrate winter!" Whittany said. "Speaking of winter, Brittany, let's get some hot chocolates."

"Yeah," Brittany added. "I need something sweet after this very sour encounter."

The Biskits trudged off, leaving deep footprints in the snow.

"What I wouldn't give to be clipped by Mr. Kenny!" Zoe swooned.

"Does he do quills?" Russell Ferguson the hedgehog asked.

Blythe refused to be star struck.

"Can't Littlest Pet Shop celebrate winter, too?" Blythe asked. "We can have a cool winter fair!"

"Awesome idea!" Russell told Blythe. "You can show your new winter pet-clothes line!"

"I'll ice sculpt!" Minka suggested.

"I'll break the ice with some jokes!" Pepper said.

"We can do something special in the store window to attract attention," Blythe said.

"Like what?" Zoe asked.

Blythe and the pets strolled through the park and saw a polar bear gliding gracefully on the frozen pond. As the bear began to twirl, Blythe smiled. "Like *that*!" she exclaimed.

Chapter 3
Polar Pair

"That's Svetlana Chillenko!" Russell said. "The famous skating polar bear from Si-*brr*-ia!"

"Look at those spins!" Vinnie gushed.

"They're making my head spin!" Sunil admitted.

"And she's not even wearing skates," Pepper said. "Pretty impressive!"

"That's why I want Svetlana to skate inside the Littlest Pet Shop window,"

Blythe declared. "We can make it look like a giant snow globe with an ice-skating rink inside!"

The moment Svetlana stepped off the ice, Blythe explained everything.

"Will you do it, Svetlana?" Blythe asked.

She and the pets held their breaths waiting for Svetlana's answer. Finally, the polar bear nodded her head.

"I will skate at your fair," Svetlana said, "under *two* conditions!"

"What? What?" the pets asked twice.

"The fair must be next Saturday," Svetlana said. "And I must have skate partner."

"Partner?" Blythe repeated.

"Like my Boris. He is still home in Si-*brr*-ia," Svetlana said, teary-eyed. "Boris is also a world-famous ice-dancing polar bear!"

"Did someone mention *dance*?" Vinnie blurted.

Disco music filled the air as Vinnie switched his wooly glove to a glittery one. As Vinnie danced, Svetlana cried out, "I have found him! I have found my new Boris!"

Chapter 4
Chills and Spills

"Come, Boris—I mean Vinnie!" Svetlana called from the ice. "Skate with Svetlana!"

"Vinnie?" Blythe whispered. "Can you dance as well on ice as on land?"

"Are you kidding?" Vinnie whispered back. "Watch me melt the ice with some hot dance moves!"

Vinnie took a flying leap. He landed on the ice, his legs in a split!

"Um . . . what . . . next?" Vinnie gulped, legs shaking.

"Start with Lutz!" Svetlana said.

"Lutz . . . no problem!" Vinnie said. He untangled his legs, put one foot forward and—

"Whoa!" Vinnie cried, sliding out of control toward Svetlana. "I *caaaaaan't stoooooopppp*!"

"I can't *watch*!" Penny said, covering her eyes.

Then Vinnie smashed right into Svetlana! The two flew high into the air before crashing to the ice in a heap!

"That was not Lutz!" Svetlana cried. "That was KLUTZ!!"

"Does that mean Vinnie isn't your new Boris?" Blythe asked as Svetlana skated to the edge of the pond.

"Not so fast," Svetlana said. "As they say in Si-*brr*-ia, practice makes perfect."

"They say that here, too!" Blythe said excitedly. "I'm sure Vinnie can get his act together by Saturday. Right, Vinnie?"

"Riiiight," Vinnie groaned as he stumbled off the ice.

"Good!" Svetlana said as she began to leave. "I'll be at Littlest Pet Shop on Saturday to skate with my new Boris!"

After waving good-bye to Svetlana, all eyes turned to Vinnie.

"Ready to practice?" Blythe asked him eagerly.

Trembling, Vinnie shook his head.

"No way am I getting back on the

ice!" Vinnie cried. "What if I fall again? What if everyone laughs at me? I won't do it! I won't do it!"

"I think that means no," Sunil whispered.

"I think Vinnie's afraid of the ice!" Pepper whispered back.

"We have to make him *unafraid* in time for Saturday's fair!" Blythe whispered.

"But how?" Zoe asked.

"Seriously . . . I don't have a clue!" Blythe admitted.

Luckily, Russell did . . .

"If *we* can't help Vinnie," Russell said, "maybe we have friends who *can*!"

Chapter 5
Shall We Trance?

Later at Littlest Pet Shop, the owner, Mrs. Twombly, was confused . . .

"Oh, Blythe?" Mrs. Twombly said, carrying a fishbowl toward the back of the store. "This fish was in front of the door without a note."

"Um . . . I'll take it, Mrs. Twombly," Blythe said, grabbing the bowl. "I won it at . . . the arcade!"

"Okeydoke," Mrs. Twombly said, heading toward the front. "Let me know if you'd like a mini-model of the Roman Colosseum for your fishbowl. They're on sale, half off."

"Mini-Roman Colosseum . . ." the fish muttered. "As if fish like that tacky stuff!"

"Everybody, may I introduce respected pet hypnotist, Dr. Helga Blowfish," Zoe said. "Helga helped me realize I was a princess in a past life."

"And present," Pepper said.

"Welcome, Dr. Blowfish," Blythe said. "Do you think you can help Vinnie?"

"I believe I can," Helga declared.

"Like how?" Vinnie said.

"Like this!" Helga said. She blinked, and then her eyes began spiraling like kaleidoscopes!

"Look into my eyes, Vinnie," Helga said. "When I flap my tail, you will be a penguin!"

"Sorry, Doc," Vinnie chuckled. "But I'm no . . . *Raaaak!*"

Blythe and the pets watched in

delight as Vinnie made penguin noises and wobbled around with his arms stiff at his sides!

"Looks like a penguin to me," Pepper said.

"That's because I am a *RAAAAK* penguin!" Vinnie declared.

"And what do penguins love more than anything, Vinnie?" Helga asked.

"Raaak!" Vinnie squawked. "They like . . . they like . . ."

"Yeeeees?" Helga urged.

"FISH!!" Vinnie exclaimed.

"Eeeek!" Helga screamed as Vinnie lunged toward the fishbowl.

"Not fish, Vinnie!" Blythe cried. "Penguins love ice! *Ice!*"

". . . Ice?" Vinnie gulped as he snapped out of his trance. "Don't make me go back on the ice and make a fool of myself. *Pleeeeeeease!*"

"We need to stop now," Helga said.

But Blythe wouldn't stop trying to help Vinnie. "Any other ideas?" she asked the pets nervously.

Chapter 6
Twist and Shout

Soon another friend slithered into Littlest Pet Shop . . .

"Yoo-hoo, Blythe!" Mrs. Twombly called. "How do you like my new boa?"

Blythe gulped when she saw Mrs. Twombly. Wrapped around her neck was a snake!

"He's a friendly corn snake," Mrs. Twombly said. "I just have no idea why he slithered through the mail slot. We don't carry snake-wear."

"I'll take him, Mrs. Twombly," Blythe said, uncoiling the snake. "It's my latest . . . um . . . zoology project!"

"Who is this guy?" Vinnie asked after Mrs. Twombly left.

"Meet Swami Twistonambra," Sunil said proudly. "He's here to teach Vinnie to relax with yoga!"

"I thought mongooses wrestled

snakes, Sunil," Pepper said.

"Only cobras," Sunil explained. "We wrestle with the meaning of life."

"Thank you for that introduction," Swami said. "Now I'd like to start the class with a few poses."

"I thought you'd never ask!" Zoe said as she struck several über-glam poses.

"I think he means yoga poses, Zoe," Blythe whispered.

Swami directed everyone to sit on the floor, then—*zip*—wound his body into a tight coil!

"I call this pose the coiled reptile!" Swami declared.

"And I call it the pretzel!" Pepper said as they tried to copy Swami. "Owie!"

After a few more poses, it was time to relax. Everyone shut their eyes and listened to Swami. "Picture yourself floating on a cloud. A fluffy cotton candy cloud."

Blythe felt relaxed,

but what about Vinnie? She glanced sideways. Vinnie's eyes were shut, a peaceful smile on his face.

"How do you feel, Vinnie?" Blythe whispered. "Are you starting to chill out?"

"Chill?" Vinnie asked. His eyes popped wide open. "Chill?!"

Vinnie jumped up. "I can't go back on the ice! I won't go back on the ice!!" he screamed.

"Bad vibes," Swami said.

"Now what?" Blythe groaned.

"What if we run out of friends who can help us?" Minka gasped.

"*Hmm*," Russell said thoughtfully.

"Maybe Vinnie doesn't need *our* friends. Maybe he needs his own friends. *Us!*"

Chapter 7
Party Animals

"Remind me why we're at the park again, Blythe?" Pepper asked. "Especially since Vinnie won't get back on the ice?"

"I told you, Pepper," Blythe said, tying on her ice skates. "We're going to lure Vinnie onto the ice with what he loves best."

"Par-tay!" Russell declared.

Vinnie stayed behind as Blythe and the pets skated onto the frozen pond. When they reached the middle, they danced to a song Zoe had written for Vinnie: *"Sand gets gritty, snow gets slushy, grass is full of mud. But everything is nice on ice when skating with your buds!"*

Everyone joined hands as Minka led a skating chain.

"See, Vinnie?" Blythe called. "We're having fun and no one is falling!"

“Won’t you join us?” Penny called.

“I don’t think so,” Vinnie said, stepping back.

“This isn’t working.” Blythe sighed. “Let’s just go back to the shop and think of a new plan.”

All the pets followed Blythe off the ice. Moments later, Pepper shouted, “Help! The ice is cracking up! And I don’t mean from my jokes!”

Blythe and the pets gasped when they saw Pepper waving her paws in the air.

“We have to help her!” Blythe cried.

"But the ice is too dangerous!" Sunil said.

Suddenly—

"Out of my way!" Vinnie shouted, running toward the pond. "I'm coming for you, Pepper!"

"Vinnie, no!" Zoe shouted.

But Vinnie was already break-dancing his way toward Pepper!

"My hero!" Pepper said when Vinnie slid to her side.

"But where's the cracked ice?" Vinnie said, looking around.

"Surprise!" Pepper said slyly.

"You mean you tricked me?!" Vinnie said.

"Hey," Pepper said. "It got you back on the ice, didn't it?"

"Yeah!" Vinnie said, shuffling his dancing feet. "And it feels great!"

Blythe and the pets felt great, too, as they skated toward Vinnie. Their friend was no longer frozen by his fear. And it was just in time for the Littlest Pet Shop Winter Fair!

Chapter 8
Bad Fair Day

It was Saturday morning, and all systems were a go for the fair.

"It's an indoor Winter Wonderland!" Blythe exclaimed as she looked around the Littlest Pet Shop.

The store was filled with Minka's ice sculptures, and even an ice cream bar with not-so-hot fudge. Snowflakes drifted from snow machines. But best of all was the window that looked like a snow globe with an ice-skating rink inside!

"Did you see the huge crowd outside?" Russell asked. "They're all

here to see Svetlana!"

"You mean, Svetlana and me!" Vinnie said, dressed in a spangled jumpsuit. "Wait till you see the routine we've been practicing!"

"Where is Svetlana?" Sunil asked. "What if she never shows up? What if she's hibernating?"

The bell over the front door jingled.

"Relax, Sunil. That's probably her," Blythe said. But when she turned, she saw Mrs. Twombly greeting a man with perfect hair and a stylist's jacket.

"Oh, no!" Blythe gasped. "That's . . . that's—"

"Blythe, I'd like you to meet Mr.

Kenny!" Mrs. Twombly said as they walked over. "From Largest Ever Pet Shop."

Blythe and the pets traded frantic looks. This was Whittany and Brittany's idea. And that meant trouble!

"Mr. Kenny is offering free trims in honor of today's fair!" Mrs. Twombly said.

"But—" Blythe started to say, until Mr. Kenny pulled a hair dryer from his satchel.

"Who's ready for a HOT new look?!"

Mr. Kenny sneered with an evil grin. He flicked on the hair dryer with a *WHIR*!

Blythe shrieked.

Mr. Kenny was blowing hot air all over the frozen store!

"No, Mr. Kenny!" Blythe cried. "*Stoooooppppppp!*"

Chapter 9
Drip, Drip, Hooray!

"What on earth are you doing?" Mrs. Twombly cried.

Mr. Kenny snickered as he turned the hair dryer on the ice sculptures, ice cream bar, and frosted trees. What was once frozen was now slush. Even

the snowflakes turned to rain. But the worst was yet to come . . .

"Not the store window!" Blythe shouted as the stylist-spy turned the ice-skating rink into a giant puddle!

"The wet look is my specialty!" Mr. Kenny sneered as he flicked off the hair dryer.

Blythe and the pets stared open-mouthed as Mr. Kenny left the store.

"I'll get a mop." Mrs. Twombly sighed as she left for the back.

"I should have known!" Blythe wailed. "I should have known that the

Biskits would ruin our winter fair!"

"Who said it is ruined?" a voice asked.

Blythe and the pets turned to see Svetlana, dressed in the sparkliest ice-skating costume ever!

"But you can't skate on a melted rink!" Blythe said.

"Polar bears swim, too," Svetlana said. "Why do you think we have paws as big as pancakes?"

"Geckos aren't bad swimmers, either," Vinnie said with a grin. "So . . . synchronized swimming, anyone?"

Soon everyone outside was cheering for Svetlana and Vinnie's magnificent performance. Blythe felt like dancing, too. A happy dance!

"So, Blythe," Russell said, "what do you think of the Littlest Pet Shop Winter Fair so far?"

"Judging from all those smiles," Blythe declared, "I'd say we made a huge, huge SPLASH!"